Usborne
Phonics Readers
Fox on a box

Phil Roxbee Cox

Illustrated by Stephen Cartwright

Edited by Jenny Tyler

Language consultant: Marlynne Grant
BSc, CertEd, MEdPsych, PhD, AFBPs, CPsychol

There is a little yellow duck to find on every page.

First published in 2006 by Usborne Publishing Ltd., Usborne House, 83-85 Saffron Hill, London EC1N 8RT, England. www.usborne.com
Copyright © 2006, 2003 Usborne Publishing Ltd.

Hungry Fox spots
a box.

2

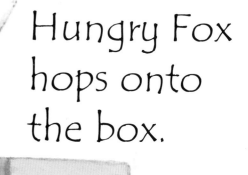

Hungry Fox
hops onto
the box.

He tries to reach...

3

Hungry Fox pushes the box.

"Now I'm as tall as the wall!" calls Fox.

5

SPLAT!

Hungry Fox
pushes the
box.

7

"I need honey from the honey bees!" says Fox.

8

Hungry Fox sits on the box.

"I want fishes,"
wishes Fox.

But a tug from Duck
means he's out
of luck.

SPLAT!

PRIZE

Hungry Fox
is on the box.

11

"I can reach the cooling pies!" cries Fox.

But Pup and
Fat Cat ...

...put a stop to that.

13

Hungry Fox falls
into the box.

PRIZE

He heaves
himself out...

...to find
cream on
his snout.

"I'm back in the box!"

shouts Happy Fox.